# CABIN CREEK MYSTERIES

# THE SECRET
# OF ROBBER'S CAVE

# THE SECRET
# OF ROBBER'S CAVE

## by Kristiana Gregory
### illustrated by Patrick Faricy

SCHOLASTIC INC.
New York   Toronto   London   Auckland   Sydney
Mexico City   New Delhi   Hong Kong   Buenos Aires

3 3113 02775 4946

ISBN-13: 978-0-439-92950-9
ISBN-10: 0-439-92950-4

Text copyright © 2008 by Kristiana Gregory
Illustrations copyright © 2008 by Scholastic Inc.
"David's Map" illustration by Cody Rutty.
All rights reserved. Published by Scholastic Inc.

12  11  10  9  8  7  6  5  4                     8  9  10  11  12  13/0

Printed in the U.S.A.                                                          40

First printing, March 2008

# CHAPTERS

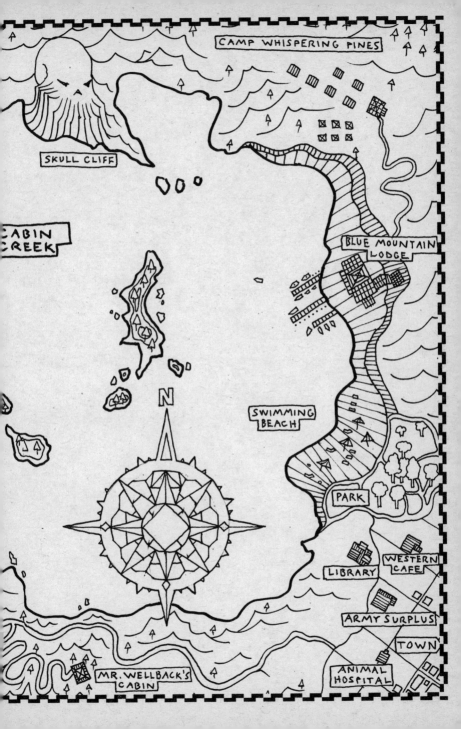

*The Cabin Creek Mysteries are dedicated to my friend,
Craig Walker, who loved a good adventure.*

*Thank you to my incredible editors Ann Reit and Kristin Earhart,
loyal cohorts and dear friends. And to editorial director extraordinaire,
Catherine Daly, who has a natural knack for mysteries.*

# 1

# Lost Island

As the canoe glided toward Lost Island, twelve-year-old Jeff Bridger dipped his paddle into the water, steering it into the inlet. Though it was summer, the air was cool. Clouds over the mountains darkened the sky. Jeff worried about a storm coming, but most of all he felt uneasy about setting foot on Lost Island.

"Let's stay together, David," he said to his ten-year-old brother. "We don't know what's out here."

This was the first time they had been out this far on the lake by themselves. Their father had always warned them to stay off the island.

*"When David turns ten, we'll all go together,"* he had said. *"But I don't want you boys out there a day before that. It's more dangerous than it looks."*

Today was David's birthday. Last night the brothers had been too excited to sleep. They had lain awake in their bunks, whispering about what they might find. They wondered about the legend, *a terrible and true tale*, their father had said. *A real robber, a cave, stolen treasure, a sheriff, and more.*

Their mother had no idea they were so far away from their cabin today. She was the town's veterinarian and would be working late at the animal hospital. She had left her sons a note, asking them to be home by sunset and to fix their own supper. They would celebrate David's birthday next week.

Jeff and David Bridger knew about the wilderness from camping with their father — a forest ranger — and because they lived several miles from town. Their log cabin was on a lake, which looked out at Lost Island. Ever since the brothers were little, they had watched this island with binoculars, hoping to find clues to its mystery — to learn why their father had declared it off-limits.

But now they would have to track down the truth themselves. It was a great sorrow that Dad was no longer there to take the boys as promised. During winters, he had worked with the ski patrol on Blue Mountain. But last December, he and another ranger had been killed in an avalanche. Thick fog, then a blizzard, had prevented rescuers from finding them for several days.

Ever since, the brothers were nervous about storms. Also, they were now more determined than ever to explore Lost Island. Uncovering the legend would help them feel close to their father.

In the canoe, the brothers wore whistles around their necks and life vests. Cell phones didn't get reception in these mountains, so they had walkie-talkies hooked to their belts. They also carried pocketknives and canteens from the army surplus store.

"Almost there!" David yelled. The younger brother always rode in the front when the boys took out the canoe. His blond hair was windblown, like straw. Rope in hand, he was ready to jump into the shallows. His daypack was below his seat in an inch of water, but he wasn't bothered by wet things. As usual, his T-shirt was inside out with the tag in front. His socks were mismatched.

The boys' dogs — Rascal, a black Scottish terrier, and Tessie, an old yellow Lab — were in the center of the canoe, like passengers on a sightseeing trip. They had sat still for the thirty-minute ride from the family's dock to the island. But at the sound of the hull

scraping against the pebbly bottom, they jumped overboard and splashed to shore.

"Stay!" the boys commanded. But their dogs ran into the woods as if chasing something. Birds flushed up from the trees with noisy chirping. Jeff suddenly felt shivery. Now that they were up close, the forest looked unfriendly, like a dark, prickly wall.

"I wonder what the dogs are after," he said. David looked uneasy. "Me, too."

They pulled the canoe onto the beach.

"Well, we're finally here," said Jeff. Then, being practical, he patted the canoe and said, "Let's turn this upside down, so it'll dry out. Then we can take a look around." He had brown hair and even though he hadn't brushed it that morning, he didn't look as rumpled as his brother. The emblem on his T-shirt read JUNIOR EXPLORERS, GRIZZLY PAW WILDERNESS. It was the name of the club started by their father, to teach kids survival skills. The shirt was Jeff's favorite.

As they tipped the water from their craft, they again called their dogs.

There was no response. This wasn't like their pets, who usually came when called.

The brothers looked up at the sky. More clouds had appeared in the north. Just then, barking pierced the air.

David swallowed hard. "That's Tessie!"

"Uh-oh," said Jeff. "It sounds like she's in trouble."

## 2

# A Grisly Discovery

The brothers ran into the woods, following their dogs' barks. They ducked under branches, climbing over rocks and rotted tree stumps.

"I think I see them. Over there!" Jeff cried. He pointed to a cluster of aspen trees.

"Tessie!" they called. "Rascal!" But the dogs did not come.

Soon the boys arrived in a small clearing surrounded by trees and bushes. To their relief, they found Rascal there. He was digging furiously with his front paws. Dirt sprayed behind him. As terriers like to do, he was shoving his nose into a hole as if sniffing out a tiny animal. He was too busy to notice the brothers.

And then they spotted Tessie. She was sitting in the shade, watching Rascal. Although she was old and plump, she still liked to retrieve things. Upon seeing the boys, she wagged her tail and came toward them. Something was in her mouth.

"Drop it," Jeff said.

Tessie dropped the object. It looked like a dirty sock with holes in it.

"What is *that*?" asked David.

Jeff leaned over for a closer look. He stared. "Is this what I think it is?"

David found a twig and pushed at it. "Yuck."

They stared and poked. Clumps of dirt fell away, revealing not a sock, but a foot with some of the anklebones attached. It was bony white, the flesh long gone. It was so old, it looked as if it would crumble with one touch.

"Is it a bear's?" David asked.

There was rustling in the trees behind them. Jeff flinched and turned. He felt as if someone were watching them.

In a whisper he said, "I think it's from a person. Looks exactly like that skeleton in the science museum."

The brothers gave each other a worried glance. They had been hoping to find *something* about the legend, but they hadn't expected human bones.

"What if this is a clue to what happened out here?" Jeff asked.

"Looks like a murder to me," said David.

For several minutes, they examined the foot. Then they kicked through Rascal's dirt pile to see if there was any other evidence. Finally Jeff pulled the small shovel from his pack and snapped the handle in place. "You can use this, David. I have a tin cup. We better dig a deeper hole for it." He nodded toward the foot.

"You mean, bury it?"

"Yeah. It might be an important clue. We can make sure it stays a secret if we leave it here."

"But why? Let's take it home so we can keep looking at it. I think it's cool."

Jeff gave his brother a long look. "David, don't forget about Claire. If she sees it, she'll start asking questions."

"Oh, yeah. I almost forgot."

Claire Posey was their nine-year-old cousin whose cabin was near theirs, just across the creek. Her parents — the boys' Aunt Lilly and Uncle Wyatt — owned the Western Café in town. Whenever they had a day off, the family spent time together, so today the Poseys were at the fairgrounds watching the rodeo.

Knowing Claire would be gone until evening was another reason why the brothers had chosen this day to visit Lost Island. Even though she was their good friend and favorite cousin, they did not want her to tag along. Not yet anyway. And it wasn't because she was a girl.

It was just that Jeff and David were not used to Yum-Yum, her new white poodle. Last month Claire had gotten her from the pound. Now wherever she went, so did Yum-Yum, wearing a collar with bells. With every step, Yum-Yum sounded like a windup toy. The boys thought the poodle was entirely too noisy to go exploring. They wanted to be as quiet in the woods as their dad had taught them to be.

"Okay," David agreed. "Let's dig that hole. Otherwise Claire will report to Aunt Lilly and Uncle Wyatt and then —"

"— and then they'll tell Mom," Jeff finished.

# 3

# Guarding a Secret

"Who could this have belonged to?" Jeff wondered.

David liked guessing. "It's got something to do with the robber and the cave," he said. "That's for sure."

Jeff and David buried the skeleton foot and patted down the dirt with their shovel. Then they rolled a heavy rock on top so the dogs wouldn't dig it up again. The rock also made a good marker. This way the boys would know where to find it so they could look at it any time they wanted to investigate more.

They retraced their steps to the beach where they felt safer. It was out in the open. They weren't wearing watches, but they could tell it was noon because the sun was overhead. In the distance, rain clouds hung over the mountain like black rolls of cotton.

"Looks like the storm is still far away," Jeff observed. He liked trying to read the sky. "Maybe there's time to —"

A twig snapped in the woods. Then another.

Slowly, the boys turned around to look. There was rustling. Something was moving in the brush.

They froze, squinting to see into the dark forest. The dogs stood beside them, ears alert.

Finally Jeff said, "Probably just a deer. That's why Tessie and Rascal aren't worried."

"You sure?"

Jeff hesitated. He reached for the walkie-talkie on his belt then clicked the switch a few times and turned a dial. "Well, let's keep these on and stick together. Just in case."

The brothers followed the creek to where there was a spring bubbling out of a rock. They filled their canteens.

"Maybe this place isn't so bad after all," said David, though he still felt uneasy. "Remember how Dad said if there's fresh water, we can survive a long time?"

"Yeah. But I wonder why he said it's more dangerous out here than it looks." Jeff was staring up a tall oak tree. Its branches were staggered like stair steps. He patted its trunk, trying to act brave. "Well, here's our lookout tower, David. Now every time we're out here, we can climb up and watch for intruders."

For twenty minutes, the boys hiked through the woods. They often stopped to see if they were being followed, but heard only the chattering of squirrels and singing of birds. At last, they reached the other side of the island. Unlike the quiet cove where they had beached their canoe, this shore was windy. Waves swept onto the rocks. Across the lake was Grizzly Paw Wilderness, miles and miles of forest and mountains. In every direction the boys saw only trees, no roads or houses.

Jeff took the compass from his pocket. "Looks like we're heading east now," he said. "This place is huge, maybe a mile long."

"Then Robber's Cave must be out here somewhere," said David.

As they rounded the tip of Lost Island, they could no longer see where the lake ended, it was so vast. The only sounds were the lapping of water and the cry of a hawk circling overhead, *kreee . . . kreee*. They were lonely sounds.

David looked at his older brother. "I wonder what Dad meant by a *terrible and true tale*. He even said it was *bloodcurdling*, remember?"

"I remember," said Jeff.

*     *     *

An hour later, the boys and their dogs had found their way back to the quiet beach. They were famished from hiking.

Jeff unzipped his pack. He liked to be prepared, so it was full of supplies. Out rolled a flashlight and a screwdriver. As he searched for his lunch, more items fell out: a first-aid kit, matches, the shovel and binoculars, dog biscuits, and a rain poncho. Finally he found the brown paper bag.

"Aha!" he said.

Now the younger boy emptied his pack. All that came out were three candy bars — soggy from the ride in the canoe — and a pencil and sketchpad, also damp.

"Where's your lunch?" Jeff asked.

"Uh . . ." David seemed surprised that he'd forgotten it. "Guess it's still in the fridge."

"What about your poncho?"

David closed his eyes as if thinking. "Maybe on the back of the couch?"

His brother shook his head. "I can't believe you forgot again. And those candy bars are too goopy to eat. Here." Jeff handed him half a cheese sandwich. It unfortunately had dropped to the ground and was squished from being in the bottom of his pack.

"Thanks," David said. When he took a bite, it crunched with sand, but he didn't mind. He was gazing across the lake at their cabin. "Hey, someone's on our porch."

Jeff stood up, sandwich in hand. He looked through his binoculars. "Uh-oh," he said.

"What?"

"It's Claire. She's holding Yum-Yum and looking this way."

"But they're supposed to be at the rodeo."

"That's what I thought," said Jeff. "I don't think she can see us, though. It's too far."

David took a swig from his canteen. He wiped his mouth with his shoulder. "But what if *she* has binocs? Didn't Mom give her a pair for her birthday?"

"No way. It was a diary or something."

"I sure hope you're right," David said. "If she finds out we came here without her, she'll explode!"

# 4

# Claire Posey

As the boys were picking up their lunch wrappers, wind suddenly filled the trees with a loud rustle. They looked up. Swift-moving clouds covered the sun. Raindrops began pelting them.

"Hurry!" Jeff yelled. "The storm's coming faster than I thought." They whistled for the dogs.

David grabbed their life vests and backpacks, then helped Jeff launch the canoe with Tessie and Rascal aboard. The boys paddled home through rough water, which soaked the sleeves of their sweatshirts. They could feel rain on their faces and down their necks.

When they turned around to look at the island, they saw a heavy fog drifting down over the trees. It was like a shroud and soon hid the shore.

Jeff yelled over the wind, "I'm glad we're off the island! That fog is freaking me out."

David paddled faster. "Me, too!"

Just as they reached the dock, lightning streaked across the dark sky, followed by a crash of thunder. The noise was fierce.

"The storm, here it comes!" Jeff cried. They ran with Rascal and Tessie to the safety of their cabin.

\*        \*        \*

A bowl of fresh blueberries was on the kitchen table with a card for David.

Happy birthday to my favorite blue-eyed son. We'll celebrate soon. I love you! Mom.

David stuck out his tongue at his brother. "I'm still her favorite," he said.

Jeff gave him a playful punch. This was a game they had played since they were little, asking their mother who she loved the most. To Jeff she always answered, "You're my favorite brown-eyed son." And, of course, David was her blue-eyed boy.

Now Jeff prepared his brother's birthday dinner: tortillas rolled up with peanut butter and bananas. They ate off paper plates and didn't set the table. It was good to be home.

"That fog on the island is spooky," said Jeff.

"The way storms come up so fast in these mountains, I'm in no rush to go back. At least for a while."

"Fine with me," David said. "Maybe there's another way to figure out the legend."

"Yoo-hoo," called a girl's voice, interrupting them.

The front door swung open and in came a jingling of bells, moving at a fast trot through the sunroom and den.

Yum-Yum entered the kitchen without looking at the boys and went straight for the dogs' bowls by the back door. Her paws clicked across the hardwood floor. She passed Tessie and Rascal, who had been sleeping. They raised their heads briefly then returned to their naps.

"What's up, guys?" Claire's curly red hair swung at her shoulders as she marched into the room. Her sweater was wet from the rain. She set a box of cinnamon Frosted Pop-Tarts on the counter. It, too, was wet.

"Happy birthday, David," she said. "These are for your dessert since you won't get cake until your party. Guess what? We had a flat tire on Cabin Creek Bridge so we never made it to the rodeo."

"Sorry to hear that," said Jeff.

David was opening the soggy box. "Hey, thanks for these. You know how I love Pop-Tarts."

"Yep, I sure do." Claire's sparkly blue head-band matched Yum-Yum's collar. Her T-shirt was green, her shorts yellow, and the laces in her hiking boots purple.

Jeff and David exchanged glances, but not because of her outfit.

Their cousin was also wearing a pair of binoculars around her neck. The official, long-range kind that rangers use to spot forest fires. Knowing Claire, she probably had been keeping track of the boys all afternoon.

She put her hand on her hip. "Our parents talked," she said. "Don't worry, you're not in trouble for going to the island without telling anyone. But here's the deal: They agreed that as long as the three of us stick together, we can go every day if we want. How 'bout tomorrow, first thing?"

Jeff took a deep breath. "Well, actually, David and I've decided —"

"Also," she continued. "I've already organized some of your favorite treats for tomorrow. But next time, turn up the volume on your walkie-talkies. I tried to reach you for hours and was getting worried. Really worried."

The brothers looked at each other. The idea of Claire coming to the island with them suddenly seemed like a good one. She was brave and dependable and she always brought snacks. They smiled at their cousin.

"It's awesome out there," Jeff said with fresh courage.

"Yeah," said David, also revived. "You'll love it, Claire."

*　　*　　*

When Yum-Yum finished inspecting the dogs' bowls, she trotted back to the den and jumped onto a couch. With her paws, she arranged a cushion so that she could rest her chin on it. Then she stared at the TV, which was off. After a moment, she looked over at Claire and barked.

"Okay, I'm coming." Claire went in and picked up the remote.

"What're you doing?" David asked.

"Yum-Yum always watches the evening news with us," Claire replied.

As the poodle made herself at home, the brothers kept quiet. They knew Claire loved the outdoors, but they guessed Yum-Yum was not going to like roughing it on Lost Island.

# 5

# The Mission

The next morning, the brothers waited on the dock for Claire, their hooded sweatshirts warm against the early chill. They wore sneakers with socks, brown from yesterday's dirt, and their T-shirts were wrinkled from having slept in them. Neither boy was fussy about his wardrobe.

As they looked across the lake to the island, they felt hopeful. The treetops were awash in sunlight. The sky was clear and their favorite cousin was coming with them. Their jitters from yesterday's storm had vanished.

"I bet Claire can help us find more clues," Jeff said.

"Me, too," said David.

After breakfast, the boys had made a caboose for their canoe. Actually, it was just an old rowboat that had been stored in their shed. Their plan was to put the three dogs in it, and all their supplies, then tow it with a rope. After hunting around their yard and garden, they found a lot of interesting junk.

Along with camping gear, they loaded the boat with a bucket of golf balls, a shower curtain, a chair, and a stool. Their toolkit had an ax for chopping wood, a hammer and nails, and a saw for trimming dangerous branches.

The largest object was part of a picket fence that David dragged out from behind the garage. It was just a few feet long, but attached to it was a little gate on hinges.

"This might come in handy," he told Claire when she arrived with Yum-Yum in her arms. Yum-Yum's nails were pink today, matching Claire's fresh nail polish.

"Are we building a clubhouse?" she asked.

"A fort," the boys answered. They didn't want to hurt her feelings, but a fort was more rugged than a clubhouse. "Claire, we'll let you pick the name, but first you have to promise us something."

"That depends," she said.

"Claire." Jeff's voice was serious. As the eldest and tallest of the three, he wanted to be a good leader. "Dad told us he had a personal mystery to solve, but we don't know what he meant. So if we keep our mission secret, just the three of us, then we can get to the bottom of the legend. There might be treasure."

"And bloodcurdling details," David added. He and his brother weren't ready to mention the buried foot. Not yet.

"Okay," she said.

David put his hand on Claire's shoulder. "So that means not telling any of your friends. Not one. Because they'll tell *their* friends; then our island will be swarming with kids, like at the mall. Get it?"

Claire raised her chin, giving each boy a queenly look. She kneeled on the dock to put Yum-Yum into the rowboat, then her pink backpack.

"*Claire?*" It was Jeff. "This is really important."

"I won't breathe a word," she said. "I *heard* you the first time."

It was almost noon by the time the kids unloaded their equipment onshore. They sat on the beach to eat their sandwiches and make plans.

David took out his pad and pencil to draw a map of the island. "See? This is where Jeff and I were yesterday." He marked an *X* with tiny arrows to show where they had hiked. "I say we look around right here." Another *X*. Then, just for fun, David made a quick sketch of their dogs — a terrier, a Lab, and a poodle — wearing party hats.

Jeff liked his brother's artwork. "Excellent idea," he said. "I'm ready."

"Then let's go," said Claire.

David folded his map into his pocket. "Onward!" he cried.

# 6

# Another Discovery

The cousins agreed to spread out. For half an hour, they crunched through the woods searching for clues.

A crackle came through Jeff's walkie-talkie. "Guys, I found something. Over."

"Where are you, Claire? Over."

"Here. To your left. Over."

Jeff and David looked up. Claire was waving to them through the trees. When she pointed to an old log cabin up ahead, the boys ran to see. It was square, with one wall crumbled down and the door missing. The wood was gray from age. Most curious of all was the pine tree growing up through part of the slanted roof. Its branches supported the beams, giving the appearance of a tree house.

"Wow!" cried David. "Can you believe it? The place looks ancient."

"Well, guys, here's our fort," said Jeff. He had to duck under a branch to enter.

As they cleared away piles of leaves and pinecones, they found what was left of a stone fireplace. A cast-iron kettle was in the rubble. Jeff looked up through the crumbling chimney.

"Let's get some mud and fix this," he said. "Then we can cook."

Even though a wall was missing, the cabin was cozy. The tree filled part of the gap, creating a natural break from the wind. And there were knotholes in its trunk where small

animals had once nested. After Claire brushed out the twigs and feathers from these holes, they made perfect little shelves. They were tiny, but she was able to fit her flashlight in one, and her compass in another. She squished a ziplock bag of Band-Aids into the smallest knothole.

"There," she said. "Home, sweet home. Who do you think lived here?"

Jeff held up a rusty trap. Its steel jaws were locked shut. "Maybe a mountain man," he answered. He handed the trap to his younger brother, who examined it carefully.

"Definitely," David said. "But Mr. Wellback would know for sure."

"Who?"

"The old man who lives up the canyon from us," said Jeff. "Everyone in town calls him Grumpy Gus, but we call him Mr. Wellback."

"Why is that?"

"It's the way he starts his stories," Jeff replied. "He always says, 'Well, back in the olden days.' Anyway, you'll see. Hey, we should ask him to tell us more about this place. Let's visit him as soon as we get home."

David said, "Okay. I just hope he's not in a bad mood again."

The cousins carried their gear to the cabin from shore, making many trips. Jeff remained watchful. So far, it seemed they were the only ones on the island.

When Tessie grew tired, Claire spread a blanket in the shade where the old dog had settled down to rest. Soon everything was stored along the walls of their fort. Jeff and David used the chair to climb onto the roof. They nailed down the plastic shower curtain around where the pine tree had grown through the shingles. Now if it rained, the cabin would be less likely to leak.

"What did Uncle Russell mean by blood-curdling?" Claire asked the boys about their father's mystery. "Is there really treasure and a robber's cave?"

"I think so," replied Jeff. "Dad said that in the olden days there was a horrible crime out here, but no one knew exactly what had happened. He wanted to find out the truth. For personal reasons, he told us."

"What did he mean by 'personal'?" she asked.

Jeff shrugged. "That's what we want to find out."

The last item brought from the rowboat was David's picket fence. It fit in the empty wall, wedged against the tree. And the gate was now their front door. Tessie, Rascal, and Yum-Yum went up to sniff it. They put their noses between the slats to look out.

David stood back to admire his work.

So did Claire. Then she offered her opinion. "I think it looks like an ice-cream stand."

"Well, I like it," David said. "And so do the dogs."

# 7

# Mr. Wellback

It was still afternoon when the cousins canoed back to their dock, towing the rowboat. Claire went home to finish her chores. The boys found a note on the fridge.

Dear sons, please clean up your considerable mess from breakfast before leaving the house again. I love you! See you tonight. Mom

"Your turn to load the dishwasher," Jeff told his brother while putting away the cereal boxes.

"No, it's your turn."

"No way," said Jeff. "I helped Mom last night while you were drawing. Remember?"

"That doesn't count. There were two of you. I'm just one."

"But there's hardly anything here."

David glared at his older brother. This was a regular debate.

"Okay, whatever," David finally said. He carried their plates to the kitchen then set them on the floor. Tessie and Rascal were waiting for him as usual. Their tails were wagging. In just a few slurps they finished the toast and jelly.

When Jeff came through the doorway, he saw David putting these plates in the cupboard.

"Mom's going to find out the dogs did the dishes," said Jeff. "She always does."

"No, she won't."

"Will, too."

"Nuh-uh."

"Well, if she *does* we'll get grounded again and what if we can't go to the island? Besides, David, it's gross."

Just then Claire and Yum-Yum made their jingly entrance. Claire saw her cousins' faces. She could tell they were arguing about chores again.

"Our parents said we have to be home by dark, remember?" she said. "And I want to meet Mr. Wellback." Without waiting for a response, she went to the mudroom for the broom and dustpan. She started sweeping the kitchen floor.

Jeff came alongside his brother and opened the dishwasher. "Here, buddy," he said, "I'll help you load. Then we can get out of here."

The cabin of Grumpy Gus was up a twisty road into the woods, a thirty-minute walk from the boys' dock. He lived by himself with several hounds and a few sneaky cats. Since he didn't have a telephone, the boys took a chance he would be there.

Howling from the hounds announced the kids' arrival as they hiked up the hill with their own dogs. The aroma of wood smoke came from Mr. Wellback's chimney. He was sitting on his porch doing a crossword puzzle. His hair and beard were white.

"What do you kids want?" he hollered as they approached.

Claire glanced at the boys, then stepped forward to introduce herself. But instead of shaking her outstretched hand, Mr. Wellback pointed to Yum-Yum's painted nails. "Since when did dogs start going to beauty parlors?"

After an awkward silence, Jeff decided to get down to business.

"Mr. Gus, sir, can you tell us more about the legend of Lost Island?" he asked.

"Sonny, that island keeps its secrets so tight, no one will ever learn the truth."

"But our dad made it sound like we could figure it out, if we tried hard enough. Did you know our father?"

"Know him? Ha!" The old man set aside his puzzle and took off his spectacles. He had the bushiest white eyebrows they had ever seen. He gazed toward the lake, his eyes serious. He drew a deep breath, but didn't speak.

The children were still standing. They looked uncomfortably at one another. After some moments Claire whispered, "Mr. Gus, are you all right?"

He turned to them. "Where was I?"

"Our father. And the legend."

"Hmph. Well, back in the olden days," he began — here, the kids smiled to hear his nickname — "there was a stagecoach robbery in Cabin Creek. Folks say the thief was wearing silver spurs on his boots. He made his getaway on a fast horse, but not before he was wounded in a bloody gun battle. Sit down there, you're making me nervous."

The cousins scrambled onto a small bench along the railing and squeezed together. They gave him their full attention, not wanting him to stop.

"Now," continued Mr. Wellback, "my great-great-grandpa was the famous gunslinger Gus Penny. Yes, I'm called Gus, too. He also was sheriff, an honorable one. Anyhow, he and his posse searched all over these parts. Do you scallywag kids know what a posse is?"

They shook their heads.

"It's a band of good guys with guns, who help enforce the law. Lots of small mountain towns still have posses these days, and they still carry rifles. Now back to the story. So, the Silver Spur Bandit disappeared. Some folks said he escaped to Canada. Others say he buried the gold on Lost Island then probably rotted to death in a cave out there."

The cousins were spellbound. Things were getting interesting. "Do you know where the cave is?" Jeff asked.

"Well, back when I was a boy, I searched and searched for it. Yessir. Found an old hunter's cabin, but no sign of the cave or any of the loot." He fell silent. Once again, his eyes seemed serious — and sad.

The children were quiet. Finally David unfolded his map and handed it to Mr. Wellback. "Sir, could you please show us where you explored?"

The old man gave the drawing a good look. Then without a word, he stood up and limped into his cabin. Through the window, the cousins saw him at his potbellied stove where he opened a little iron door. He looked over his shoulder at the kids, then tore up David's map. He threw it into the flames. When Mr. Wellback returned to the porch, he wagged his finger at them.

"If I were you," he said, "I'd stay away from that island. It's been nothing but trouble around here. Understand?"

Jeff and David nodded. Claire scooped up Yum-Yum and held her to her chest.

Mr. Wellback leaned so close, they could see his yellow teeth. In a low voice he said, "They don't call it Lost Island for nothing."

# 8

# A New Worry

The next day, the cousins rode their bikes to town. It was several miles away, so they took a shortcut through the woods. They left old Tessie at home with Rascal to keep her company, but Yum-Yum got to ride in the basket on Claire's handlebars. The poodle's frizzy white ears flapped in the breeze, and her bell jingled over every bump. When they arrived at the Western Café, Yum-Yum curled up in the basket to nap.

Aunt Lilly greeted them. She was plump and pretty, with red hair like her daughter. Uncle Wyatt wore cowboy boots and a cowboy hat, even when he was cooking.

"Glad to see you darlings," said Aunt Lilly with a warm smile. "Have you eaten lunch?"

"Not yet."

"Well, then, you better sit yourselves down," said Uncle Wyatt. He led them to a booth in the corner where a window looked out on Main Street. It was the perfect place to talk. "The usual?" he asked.

"Yes, please!"

After he left for the kitchen, the cousins leaned close to one another.

"I say we go to the island anyway," Jeff said in a whisper. His brown eyes were determined as he glanced around the diner. He didn't want the teenagers at the nearby table to hear their conversation.

"Me, too," said David, also whispering. He unfolded a new map that he had drawn, pointing out the fort and where they had already hiked. "What if Mr. Wellback's just trying to scare us? Maybe he really knows where the cave is and where the gold is buried. That's why he wants us to stay away."

"That doesn't make sense," Claire said. Her voice was quiet, too. "Why wouldn't he just dig up the treasure? I don't think he knows. Even if —" She stopped talking when she recognized two boys from school staring at her. They were at the counter ordering takeout.

The cousins were quiet until the boys left with bags of french fries. As they left, one of the boys turned around and glared at Claire. It was the school bully, Ronald McCoy. As always, Claire ignored him.

"But Mr. Wellback made it sound dangerous. What kind of trouble was he talking about?" asked David, still whispering.

"Probably a murder," said Jeff, "or a terrible accident. Hey, why do you think Mr. Wellback acted annoyed when we mentioned Dad?"

"I was wondering that, too," David said.

"Same here," said Claire. "Well, whatever happened at the island, we can find out at the library. My teacher said they have old newspapers from pioneer days. But first, why don't we get some supplies and fix up the fort more?

The dogs can protect us. And even if it takes all summer to find the cave, we'll at least have a secret hideout."

Jeff and David smiled at their cousin. She had the hang of things.

After lunch, they pedaled their bikes to the end of Main Street. They turned down a dirt road and stopped in front of their favorite store, Cabin Creek Army Surplus. They had come here often with Dad, to buy goose-down sleeping bags and other camping gear. The place had a rich aroma of canvas and leather.

They searched the aisles, Yum-Yum in Claire's arms. Soon they found what they needed — large pulleys and nylon rope — then went to the cash register. From their pockets, they counted out the money they had earned doing odd jobs.

"Thank you," they said to the teenage clerk. As he put their items in a large plastic bag, he eyed them with suspicion. His name was Rex McCoy and his father owned the store. His brother had been one of the kids at the diner's take-out counter. The cousins tried to hurry away, but Rex held on to the bag.

"You're up to something," the teenager said. "I can tell." With his free hand, he took a chocolate bar from the candy rack, opened it with his teeth, then spit its wrapper on the floor.

"We're just loyal customers," said David. "Out for some fresh air." He had heard this on a TV commercial and liked the sound of it.

"Out for fresh air, huh? Sure. And I'm

Santa Claus." Rex bit into the chocolate and chewed with his mouth open, smacking his lips. "My little brother said he saw you guys at the café, reading a map and whispering. Acting sneaky and stuff. Said he heard something about a cave. That it's on one of the islands out on the lake."

Claire looked Rex in the eye. "Your brother Ronald was in my class. He knows I like maps and that I like to hang out with my cousins." Claire paused as she shifted Yum-Yum under her arm. "Now, if you're done bothering us, we'll be on our way." She stood on her tiptoes to reach over the counter, pulling on the bag until Rex let go.

"I'll figure out what you shrimps are doing," Rex called after them. "You and your stupid dog."

*   *   *

Before riding home, the kids parked their bikes in front of the small grocery store by the marina. This was where tourists and fishermen bought supplies before going camping or out on the lake. The boys liked the noise and gasoline smell of motorboats because it reminded them of being with Dad. They also liked watching the docks as people came and went, most of them happy to be in the mountains on a sunny day.

The boys made their own fishing poles out of sticks they found on the ground. Claire sat on the dock reading. After two hours, they remembered their grocery list.

"I'll stay here with the bikes," Claire volunteered.

Jeff took a scrap of paper from his pocket. "Mom wants us to get a cake mix for David's birthday party tonight and some hotdogs. Be right back."

While the brothers were in the store, Claire noticed two familiar figures approach the marina. They wore daypacks and were looking at a map together. She stood up to see better.

*Rex and Ronald McCoy! What were they doing?* she wondered. She watched them get into a dinghy, which was a rubber boat with an outboard engine. Rex pulled the string to start the motor then revved it good and loud, churning the water. Just as they were speeding away, Jeff and David came out of the market with their purchases.

Claire was pointing at the lake. "The McCoy brothers," she said. "I don't trust those two.

Ronald always caused trouble in class and once he even made our teacher cry."

The cousins stared at the departing boat. A silvery piece of paper flew into the air then down to the water. "Looks like Rex is eating another candy bar," David said.

"Yeah," said Jeff. "And I bet they're going searching for our treasure. Come on!"

They pedaled home along a woodsy path that skirted the lake. They could see the McCoys' boat slowing down around the inlets and other islands.

"I'm glad Lost Island is so far from town," Claire said. "Maybe they'll get bored before they make it there."

# 9

# Fixing Up the Fort

David's birthday party was a barbeque on the beach in front of their cabin. The cousins kept glancing across the lake and listening for the sound of a motorboat. So far, there was no sign of the McCoy brothers.

Dr. Daisy Bridger was blond like David, and tall. She wore blue jeans with a western shirt, and her hair was in a long braid over her shoulder. "Happy birthday, sweetheart," she said, handing David his gift. It was wrapped in newspaper and tied with string. She was practical as well as thrifty.

"Thanks, Mom!" David hugged her after ripping away the paper. Inside was a new sketchbook. It was zipped into a waterproof case with colored pencils, perfect for canoe travel and mapping Lost Island.

He couldn't wait to get over there. But the next morning, chores kept the cousins in town. Their job was to arrange bricks at the Western Café, for its new outdoor patio. It was hard work and took three days. Uncle Wyatt and Aunt Lilly paid them each twenty dollars.

Finally, they were able to return to the island's quiet cove.

"I just hope the McCoys never made it," Jeff said after they beached their canoe.

The cousins hurried to the fort. The picket gate was open, but otherwise nothing seemed amiss. When they noticed a cluster of footprints below their lookout tower, then a candy wrapper trapped in the brush, Claire stomped her foot.

"I knew it," she cried. "Rex and Ronald *have* been here. It's just like them, not to pick up their trash. Now those boys are going to bother us all summer, searching for the cave."

David put the litter in his backpack. "Well, let's hope they didn't see our fort. Then they won't know this is the right island."

"Yeah," Jeff added. "If they don't find the treasure right away, I bet they'll give up."

*    *    *

The cousins made a table by rolling in an old log they found in the clearing. They could tell it had been used long ago as a chopping block because there were all kinds of cuts from an ax on the top. Set upright, it was large enough for them to spread out their sandwiches and bag of chips. For seating they used a smaller log, the chair, and the stool. Then they hung their sweatshirts, canteens, and other gear on the little branches of their pine tree. With all the dangling gadgets, it was as colorful as a Christmas tree.

By the fireplace, they stacked kindling in case they should want a fire. Even in the summer, the mountains could turn cold.

Finally Jeff and David decided it was time to build a platform in their lookout tower, which was near the cabin.

"We'll be up high enough to survey the island," they told their cousin. "And search for other clues."

"I'll stay here with the dogs." Claire wanted to organize things and ponder a proper name for their fort.

The oak was one of the tallest trees on the island, its branches thick and easy to climb. In their backpacks, the brothers carried hammers and nails and some small boards. The higher they went up the trunk, the more sway they felt from the wind. They hung on tight.

"What a view!" Jeff cried.

"Totally! I didn't know the lake was so big," said David. His blond hair blew around his face.

The water was turquoise, reflecting the sky, and most of the shoreline was forest. The other islands were also dark with pine. From their perch, the boys could see the Blue Mountain Lodge and its ski hill in the distance. Streams looked like silver ribbons curling through ranches and farmland. The town of Cabin Creek resembled a miniature train set with tiny stores and tiny cars. Their mom's animal hospital was a tiny box near the park. And nearby was the Western Café.

Jeff and David set to work. They hammered boards around the upper trunk, but not into the bark itself. Their father had taught them how to do this without nailing into the bark, which would hurt the tree. Soon they had seats, safely wedged onto the sturdy limbs. There was room for David to draw on his sketchpad. And they could sit comfortably with their binoculars.

Next, they looped a long section of rope around a branch. To this they attached a pulley, which they nailed onto their platform. Jeff climbed down to the ground then went to the fort. Onto the cabin's roof he nailed another pulley. Now the rope looked like a telephone wire stretching up to the tower.

Jeff climbed back up to the platform. He called Claire on his walkie-talkie even though they were close enough to hear each other shout. Pushing a button, he said, "Delivery system ready. Over."

Her voice came through the crackling noise. "Be right there. Over."

A few minutes later the boys saw the rope moving, inch by inch. The pulley creaked and squeaked. Soon a bucket appeared. Inside was a small jug of lemonade. Missing its cap, much of it had sloshed out. David set it beside him then returned the pail. More creaking and up came a bag of potato chips. They were crumbly, but the boys didn't mind. There was nothing like a snack after hard work.

"Mission accomplished," Jeff said to Claire. "You and the dogs okay down there? Over."

"Of course," she answered. "I finally have a name for our fort. But there's something you have to see. The sooner you guys get down here, the better. Over."

# ⑩
# New Clues

Jeff and David climbed down the tree in a hurry. Claire was pacing in front of the fort with the folding shovel. Her red hair shone in the sunlight.

"Claire, what's wrong?" they asked, throwing their packs to the ground.

"I think I found a clue! Sorry to worry you but . . . well . . . you'll see. Hurry!"

Inside the cabin by the fireplace, she poked the shovel into some soft dirt. "I was digging

where we found that old kettle and saw this."
With the spade, she lifted what appeared to be
the lid to a box. The wood was rotten.

"Wow!" cried David. "Is there more?"

"Yes. That's why I wanted you guys here.
Something else is buried. Maybe together we
can dig it up without things falling apart."

"It's the treasure," said David. "I knew it."

"Then let's be careful." Jeff wasn't as quick
to jump to conclusions.

With two shovels and a tin cup, the cousins carefully scraped away dirt and began
digging. At last they were able to lift out the
remains of a small wooden chest the size of a
shoe box. They set it on their table and stared.

"What is it?" they asked one another.

Claire unzipped her pack and took out her
hairbrush. "First, let's wipe away the dust."

Using her brush as a little broom, she uncovered a small metal wheel. It had sharp edges and was attached to what looked like an iron horseshoe. There were two of these objects inside the chest.

The cousins took turns examining them. They were heavy.

"Spurs!" cried David.

Jeff laughed out loud. "All right! Silver spurs. Just like Mr. Wellback said. Boy, are they tarnished." While the brothers gave each other high fives, Claire felt inside the box. She pulled out part of a newspaper, the *Cabin Creek Gazette*. It was brittle, and tore when she unfolded it.

"Look, guys. This is from 1882." She started reading:

**CABIN CREEK GAZETTE**

JULY 10, 1882

# Wells Fargo Driver Killed
## On Main Street
# $12,000 MISSING

## SILVER SPUR BANDIT
## STILL ON THE LOOSE

*Hand Shot off in Bloody Gun Battle*
## REWARD
## DEAD OR ALIVE
SHERIFF GUS PENNY & POSSE SEARCHING

"Wow," said David. "Twelve thousand bucks. So this was the robber's secret chest! His spurs are here, but where's the treasure?"

"Maybe it's buried in this cabin," Claire replied. "Or Robber's Cave, if we ever find it."

But Jeff had noticed something odd. "Read that again, Claire. About the gun battle."

"Mm, let's see. It says the bandit's hand was shot off."

Jeff and David fell silent.

"What's wrong?" she asked.

Jeff looked at his brother. "We were getting ready to tell you —"

"Tell me what?"

The boys talked at once. "We already found a clue . . . the first day we got here . . . a human foot, totally gross . . . we buried it so no one else would steal it. . . ."

Claire seated herself on the stool and smiled. "Wow," she said. "So you really found a person's foot? Do you think it belonged to the Silver Spur Bandit?"

"Definitely," said David. "I'm sure of it now."

"Wait a sec." Jeff took a long drink from his canteen then screwed on the cap. "The article says it was a hand, not a foot."

"Then it's a mistake," David said, sure of himself. "Mom's always showing us typos and bad grammar in the newspaper."

"So the bandit lost his *foot?*" asked Claire. "Not his *hand*? You think the *Gazette* was wrong?"

David nodded. "Absolutely."

Jeff was more cautious. "Maybe," he said.


While eating their sandwiches, Claire suddenly jumped off her stool. "Oh! I almost forgot your surprise! The name of our fort."

Both boys took a breath. They *had* promised Claire she could choose the name.

"*Ta-da!*" announced Claire. "It's Fort Grizzly Paw. In honor of the club your dad started. And also because Grizzly Paw Wilderness is across the lake. I think it's a good name for this place, don't you?"

Jeff looked at her with a smile. "You really thought about this," he said. "I like it."

"Me, too," said David. "I'm glad it's not Fort Rosy Sunshine Face or something splashy like that."

"David." Claire put her hand on her hip and rolled her eyes. "You're silly. How did you know that was my second choice?"

To keep their discoveries a secret, the cousins hid the old chest at home. They buried it and the spurs in David's closet, under a pile of shoes and comic books. Claire placed the news-paper article inside of a book to keep it flat.

"Maybe we should give this stuff to the museum," Jeff said.

"Can't we wait a while?" asked David. "If other people know, they'll all come to Lost Island looking for treasure."

"I know. Let's go to the library first," Claire suggested. "If we can find an old prospector's map, then —"

"Then we can get to the cave first," said David. "Before the McCoy brothers and everyone else."

# 11

# A Suspicious Customer

The library was in the center of town, next to the park and baseball field. The cousins left their bikes and Yum-Yum under a shady tree then went inside. Claire led Jeff and David to the map section upstairs.

"My teacher took our class here," she said. "There're atlases from all over the place. The ones for Cabin Creek are on this shelf. Let's start here."

They carried several of the oversize books

to a table by a window. From their seats they could look out at the town. While Claire turned the large pages, searching for a chart of Lost Island, the brothers kept gazing out at the blue sky. On this sunny day, they would rather be on the island, looking for the cave in person. But Claire had insisted they come to the library first. She liked to do research before jumping into things.

A deep voice startled them. "What're you kids doing?" It was Mr. Wellback with an armful of books. One of them was a dictionary for crossword puzzles. He was wearing a plaid shirt, blue jeans, and sneakers. Scowling, he limped over to their table. When he looked down at Claire's atlas, his bushy white eyebrows seemed alive.

"Hmmgh," he grunted. "Still hunting for a cave, I see. I thought I told you rabble-rousers to stay off that island."

"But we just want to know what Dad was going to tell us," said Jeff. He tried to sound older than his twelve years.

"You are not going to find a map of it here, that's for ding-dong sure." Mr. Wellback turned away, mumbling under his breath. "And I'm glad you won't."

He started down the stairs, holding on to the rail to steady himself. But he turned around to glare at the boys. "Does your mom know where you are?" His voice was loud for being in a library. He turned to Claire. "And your parents?"

"Yes, Mr. Gus," said Claire.

"We always leave a note," the brothers answered.

The old man waved his hand as if shooing flies, then he hobbled away.

The cousins stayed at the table. Claire continued to examine the colorful pages of maps. But Jeff and David had discovered a book on fighter jets. The photographs were more thrilling than the atlases. David took out his sketchpad and started drawing an air battle with rockets and parachutes.

"Cool," said Jeff. "Now do one with a Russian MiG."

David filled up eight pages, making a cartoon strip.

"Keep going," said Jeff.

"Guys," Claire interrupted. She pointed out

the window to the street below. A row of parked cars was in front of the hardware store. They could see Mr. Wellback's white hair and white beard as he carried some lumber over his shoulder to his blue pickup truck. Coils of rope were around his chest, like a cowboy's lariat. He was walking briskly.

"He sure seems strong," said Claire.

"Well, that makes sense. He's from a long line of mountain men," Jeff said. "So?"

"But look! He's not limping anymore," she answered. "When he was here fifteen minutes ago, he was stooped over and grouchy. Remember?"

David was sharpening his pencil with his thumbnail. "Yeah," he said. "That's weird. Now it looks like he's smiling."

The cousins watched Mr. Wellback make two more trips from the hardware store to his truck. Then he drove away.

Now Jeff and David were curious about something. They went to the periodical section and located the newspapers from the 1800s. They found copies of the *Cabin Creek Gazette* bound inside large black books. The pages were photocopies, not the delicate originals. Still, they looked old enough. Jeff and David studied issues from the year 1882.

After several minutes of reading, they looked at each other.

Jeff spoke in a low voice. "Mr. Wellback's ancestor was in on the robbery! He planned the whole thing."

"Wow," said David. "So the old sheriff was a bad guy, not a hero."

"What're you talking about?" asked Claire from across the table.

David explained the article to her. "Gus Penny and his posse disappeared with the Silver Spur Bandit! No one ever saw them again. Or any of the loot. Mr. Wellback lied to us."

Jeff thought a moment. "Well, maybe he doesn't want us to learn the truth. I'd feel weird if our grandpa was a villain, too."

"Here's another problem," Claire said. "Look at this." Five atlases were opened to the section for Cabin Creek, with maps of the town and lake.

"Do any of them show the cave?" Jeff asked.

She shook her head. "No. All the maps of Lost Island are missing."

"What!" he cried in a loud whisper.

"You're kidding," said David.

"Nope. Not kidding." Claire showed her cousins where pages had been torn out. "Someone else must be trying to solve the mystery."

David whispered, "I wonder who?"

"Maybe someone who likes to solve puzzles," said Jeff, remembering Mr. Wellback's crossword puzzle dictionary. "Or someone who doesn't want us to find the cave."

The cousins looked out the window. Mr. Wellback was probably home by now.

\*        \*        \*

The librarian sitting at the reference desk was new. Claire had never seen her before. She showed the woman the damaged books.

"See?" Claire said. "Someone stole these pages."

The librarian looked over her shoulder, then pushed the books aside. She was blinking and would not look at Claire. "Well, what d'you expect me to do?" she asked. "Produce the missing maps out of thin air?"

"No, ma'am, I just thought —"

"Run along now, little girl. I'm swamped here with more pressing details." She turned to a stack of magazines by her computer.

Back at the table, the cousins kept their eyes on the librarian.

"She sure seems nervous," David whispered. "She keeps looking all around."

The woman picked up a phone and punched the keypad to make a call. While speaking in a low voice, she watched the children.

"Why is she staring at us?" Jeff asked. "She's acting kind of suspicious."

Claire nodded. "I think she knows something."

"I bet you're right," agreed David.

# 12

# In a Hurry

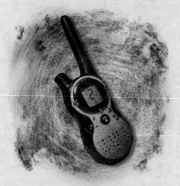

The next morning, Jeff and David were eating breakfast in their kitchen nook. They could see across the creek to Claire's log house. Uncle Wyatt was backing his jeep out of the driveway.

David's spoon paused over his cereal bowl. "There goes Claire," he said.

Jeff was spreading peanut butter on his toast. "Too bad she and Yum-Yum will be gone until dinner."

The brothers looked at each other. They were thinking the same thing.

"Now's our chance," said David. "We can do some exploring *our* way."

Jeff didn't want their cousin to feel left out, but he was tired of research. And he didn't want to be stuck at their cabin all day. "Yeah," he said. "What're we waiting for?"

With just two boys and two dogs, the canoe sailed swiftly over to the sandy cove. Jeff and David wore baseball caps to keep the sun out of their eyes. So far, it was the hottest day of June.

The fort was shaded by the pine tree growing through its roof. Because summer heat was hard on old Tessie, the brothers put her inside with Rascal so she wouldn't be lonesome. They went to the spring to fill their canteens and the dogs' drinking bowl.

Packs on their backs, they closed the picket gate. Even though the lookout tower was just a short hike away, the boys stopped to listen. Blue jays squawked from the trees, and a pair of squirrels chased each other through the brush.

"That noise is just animals," Jeff said. "I don't think the McCoy boys are out here. We would've heard their outboard motor. And their loud voices. I bet they haven't been back since that first time."

"I hope you're right," said David.

The lookout tower was easier to climb now that they were used to it. When they reached the platform, they took out their binoculars. They felt anxious as they scanned the island for intruders. They could see their canoe on the beach, but no other boats on the lake.

However, on the far shore there was someone standing on the dock by their house — it was an old man with binoculars.

"Mr. Wellback!" David cried. "He's been watching us. We better hurry and find the cave before he decides to come out here."

Jeff pointed to a cluster of bushes below. "What about that boulder that looks like a hill? There could be a cave around there. Let's check it out again."

"Yeah!" David stretched his leg down to the next branch and began his hurried descent. Jeff followed. Twice Jeff stepped on his brother's hand by accident, but David didn't complain.

Explorers didn't worry about such small matters.

A few minutes later, the brothers stood before a wall of brush and scrub pine. They were drinking from their canteens. The heat had made them thirsty. They hadn't been wary of Lost Island since that first day with the storm, but now Jeff was uneasy again. Rain clouds had suddenly darkened the sky. A breeze was stirring up dirt.

Just then a candy wrapper fluttered in the wind. It crossed their path and became trapped in the underbrush.

"Oh, no!" David cried. "The McCoys *were* here!" Trying to track down the proof, he crawled after the wrapper. Only the bottoms of his sneakers were visible as he disappeared.

A moment later, David yelled for his brother. His voice echoed as if he were in an empty room. "Quick! You won't believe this."

On hands and knees, Jeff followed under the scratchy boughs of a spruce tree. Down a slope, he finally reached David and stood up. Before them was a narrow opening to a cavern. It was dark and they could feel cool air coming from within.

"Is this really it?" they asked each other. "No wonder it was hard to find."

Suddenly the sky flashed with lightning.

They hurried to stand in the safety of the cave's deep entrance. A loud rumble of thunder was soon followed by rain.

"Whew," Jeff said, taking off his cap. "At least it's dry here."

"Think we should go in if there's a storm?" David wondered.

"Well, it's too dangerous to canoe home right now," Jeff reminded him. "And we're here. We may as well have a look."

"Okay. I guess so."

"Let's make sure we're ready. Got your flashlight? Here's mine."

David rummaged through his pack. "Check," he said, clicking his on.

"What about your sketchpad and pencil, so we can map out this place?"

"Check."

"Canteens?"

"Check," they both answered.

"Walkie-talkies?"

"Check," they again answered.

"Trail mix?"

"Check."

"Chocolate?"

"Uh . . . how about red licorice?"

"That'll do. Let's go."

"You first!" cried David.

And into the cave they went.

# 13

# Twists and Turns

The boys' flashlights revealed stone walls that were cool to the touch. The ceiling was just tall enough for them to stand without bumping their heads. A sharp, musty odor stung their eyes.

"Something smells bad," David said. "It's giving me the creeps! Do you think it's a bear? Or a dead body?"

"I hope not!" said Jeff. "And I hope it's not the stinkin' McCoy boys." He shone his light to where the path split into two directions. "Let's go here."

David paused. "Okay. But go slow. I don't want to meet a grizzly."

The smell grew stronger as they followed twists and turns of the narrow path. Something crunched underfoot. David shone his flashlight to the ground.

"Gross! What are those?" he asked.

Jeff bent down to look. "I think they're rat droppings. Are those little bones?"

"Eew," David replied.

Just then, a loud flurry of wings whooshed overhead. The brothers yelled as they felt the wings graze their scalps. Ducking, they saw hundreds and hundreds of bats, squeaking like mice. The boys crouched low and threw their arms overhead. But still they could feel

prickles as the tiny mammals scraped their shoulders before flying into the darkness.

"Yuck!" the boys cried.

"Maybe we should turn back," David said.

Jeff rubbed his hair to get rid of something sticky. "Five more minutes, please, David?"

"I guess so," said the younger boy. "But I don't like it in here."

When it was quiet again, their courage returned.

"Wonder where the Silver Spur Bandit went hiding?" Jeff yelled to hear his voice echo.

"Me, too," David hollered, swinging his arms. "I wonder how he got away on his bloody stump!"

"The McCoys probably ran home crying when they saw all those bats!"

"Babies!"

"Yeah," they both shouted.

Suddenly Jeff's flashlight began to blink. He tapped it against his palm. It blinked two more times, then it went out. Now the walls of the cave seemed to close in around them.

"I knew we should've brought extra batteries," Jeff said. "At least yours works."

David was still feeling brave. "Hey, Jeff, watch this." He put his light under his chin. The glow shining up cast his face in frightening shadow. In a low voice he said, "Yo ho ho and a bottle of rum."

"Cut it out, David. We need to turn around and —"

"Shh. What was that?"

"What d'you mean?"

"I heard something."

"I told you to cut it out."

"No, I'm serious." David was whispering.

*Skeecht . . . skeecht . . .*

"There! That scratching sound. Hear it now? Maybe the McCoys are still here."

A new noise startled them. A high-pitched howling. They grabbed each other.

*Whooo . . . whooo . . . whooooo-ooh . . .*

David felt goose bumps on the back of his neck. "I hope that's just the storm!" he cried.

"Let's get outta here!" yelled Jeff.

"I'm right behind you!"


Hurrying, the brothers retraced their steps to the entrance of the cave. But it was dark where the opening had been. There was no warm air or sunlight. Something was blocking their way. They could hear wind shrieking down a distant corridor.

Out of breath from running, they tried to gather their thoughts. David stood back to give his flashlight a wide view. They were staring at a barricade made from logs roped together. Jeff pushed, but it didn't budge.

"I can't believe it!" he cried, pounding on the wood. "Someone trapped us in here."

"But who?" David kicked it with his foot. "Who knows we're here?"

The boys fell silent. A trickle of dirt fell from overhead, splashing into a puddle. Somewhere down the long tunnel, a tiny animal scurried away.

"Rex and Ronald!" said David. "They've been watching us the whole time."

"Or —"

"Or who?"

"Or Mr. Wellback," Jeff answered.

"Huh," said David. "So *that's* why he was buying all that rope and wood. We were right about him. He doesn't want us to find any gold."

"Probably," Jeff said, nodding. "And now that I think about it, the McCoys couldn't have built this barricade so fast. Even though their dad owns the surplus store, they're lazy."

"Yeah, lazy loudmouths," agreed David, his hands on his hips. "So now what?"

Jeff took off his pack and brought out his walkie-talkie. He clicked it on, turning a dial. "Claire Posey," he said. "Come in, Claire. Over."

There was no sound. Not even a crackle.

Jeff tried again. Then David tried his.

"No reception," said Jeff. "This tunnel is like a tomb."

"Well, I better save our batteries." David snapped off his flashlight. The complete darkness was as if a hood had been pulled over their heads. It was so black they blinked and blinked, but could see nothing.

"At least we left Mom a note. She'll send a search party."

"But she won't be home until two in the morning. What should we do until then?"

"First off, we have to stay calm."

"Okay."

"And not panic."

"I don't care about the legend anymore."

"Me, neither."

"Dad would say we should've prepared better," David admitted. "He never would have come into a cave without good, solid plans, and letting people know where he was."

"Neither would Claire."

"You're right. I wish we had waited for her."

# 14

# Trapped

The brothers sat in the darkness. Though it was summer, they were getting cold leaning against the stone wall. The cave felt chilly and damp, as if it had never seen sunlight. There was now a dreadful sound nearby: the *drip-drip-drip* of water.

"Jeff, the ground feels like it's getting wet. What if this place floods? We'll drown."

"I don't think the dripping will cause a flood, David."

"Well, we've gotta do something. I'm turning on my light, okay?"

There was a click, then brightness. They squinted.

"All right," said Jeff, scuffling to his feet. "We've been sitting here long enough. Let's do like on the cop shows and kick in this door."

"Yeah! On the count of three?"

David propped the flashlight so it shone on the barricade. "Ready."

"Okay. One! Two! Three!" The boys raised their knees to their chests and gave the door a sideways kick. Nothing happened.

"Again!" They counted, then kicked as hard as they could. There was a creak in the wood. They kept at it until a strand of rope loosened, then split apart. Logs tumbled to the ground. The noise rumbled through the tunnel.

But instead of sunlight and trees on the other side, there was more darkness.

"Where are we?" Jeff said. "This isn't where we came in. And this barricade is just a bunch of old wood with rotting rope. It's probably been here for ages. Mr. Wellback didn't do this. And neither did the McCoys, that's for sure."

David pushed at the logs until he was able to step through. His foot splashed in a puddle. "Hey, this is some kind of room." He shone his light. The wall was wet.

Now David's light began to flicker . . . flicker . . . flicker. Then it went out completely. He switched it off and on several times. "Uh-oh," he said. "Jeff, I can't see you."

"Hold on. I'll get my matches." There was a rattling as Jeff went through his pack. Soon, a flare lit up his face. The small flame was comforting, but lasted only ten seconds. It scorched his fingers as it burned out.

"Can I try?" David asked.

"Okay. Here. But be careful. We need them to find our way back to the entrance."

David made a grand display of striking his match and waving it in the air. But when its flame started burning his hand he yelled, "Ouch!" And once again it was dark.

A moment passed.

"David? You okay?"

"Yeah."

"Well, what's the matter? Why don't you light another?"

"I dropped them."

"So? Pick 'em up."

"Um, there's a puddle."

"You mean —?"

"I'm sorry, Jeff. The matches are sopping wet."

# 15

# Total Darkness

The blackness reminded the brothers of a game they used to play. They would take turns hiding in their bedroom closet. Whoever stayed in the longest without getting scared was the winner. But today wasn't a game.

"This is freaking me out," said David.

"Same here."

"Maybe we should try to go backward,

Jeff. I bet we'd find the entrance after a while."

"But it's too dark. Another wrong turn and who knows where we'd end up? Remember how Dad always told us to stay in one place if we get lost?"

"Okay."

After a while Jeff said, "Hey! Do you see that?"

"What?"

Jeff was pointing in the darkness to a small light overhead. At first he thought it was a firefly, because it appeared to be moving. But when he tried to touch it, it was beyond his reach.

"David," he said. "Does that look like a hole to you? In the ceiling?"

The brothers stared for a moment.

"Yeah."

"Here, I'll boost you up." With an *oomph*, he lifted the smaller boy.

"Oh, wow," David cried. "I can see trees and blue sky. Looks like it stopped raining."

"Try to make the hole bigger," said Jeff. "Maybe we can climb out."

David put his fist through and scratched at the dirt outside. Pebbles and soggy pine needles spilled onto their heads. "Jeff, let me down. I have an idea!"

In the darkness, the brothers searched their packs until they found their pocketknives. For twenty minutes, they took turns holding each other on their shoulders. They chiseled at the hole, but made little progress.

"Solid granite. At this rate, it'll take us years." Jeff sighed with frustration.

"Well, I just want to get out of here," David said. "What if no one ever finds us?"

Jeff swallowed hard. He didn't want to scare his younger brother by admitting that he, too, was nervous.

The ray of sunshine slanted down into the darkness. The boys sat in its pool of light. They could hear wind in the trees outside. Ravenous, they ate some licorice and shared Jeff's banana sandwich. Their canteens were almost empty.

\*　　\*　　\*

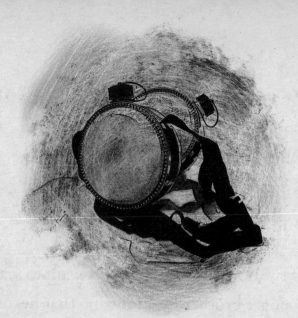

As the afternoon passed, the spot of sunshine slid up the wall, then disappeared. Now it was night. A star twinkled overhead and they heard crickets.

"You cold?"

"Freezing. It's damp in here. That water's still dripping somewhere."

"Rub your arms fast, then your legs. It helps warm you up."

"Okay. How long do you think we've been in here?"

"Hours."

"At least here we have a tiny bit of light and fresh air. And Mom's on duty until two A.M., so she should be coming home soon. She'll see our note, then —"

"Jeff?"

"What?"

There was a rustling as David dug in his backpack for a piece of paper. He handed it to his brother. "When we were looking for our knives, I found this."

Jeff held it up to the starlight. "Our note to Mom?" he questioned. "What's it doing here?"

"We left in such a hurry. I guess I

accidentally shoved it into my bag with my art stuff. I'm sorry, Jeff."

"It's okay, buddy. I was in a hurry, too. I wanted to get out here and really find something."

David sneezed. He was shivering. "Our poor dogs," he said. "Rascal worries when we're not around and old Tessie gets cold so easy. They haven't had dinner, either."

"Well, at least they're keeping each other company."

"Yeah. Like us."

# 16

# An Unexpected Visitor

Jeff bolted awake. It was pitch-dark.

*Where am I?* he wondered. Then he felt his brother's shoulder next to his. *The cave. We're still here.*

"David?" He shook the younger boy's arm. "Hear that?"

They looked up to the circle of starlight. How many hours had passed, they couldn't tell. They listened. A faint jingling was coming from outside. It was getting louder.

"Is that Yum-Yum?" They grabbed each other, straining to hear. It seemed impossible.

"Yum-Yum!" they cried.

"How'd Claire get on the island?"

"Who cares? Here, I'll lift you," said Jeff. "Call her. Loud as you can."

Up went David. He yelled their cousin's name. The jingly bells stopped. He could see Claire's light flash against the dark trees overhead.

"Jeff! David!" came Claire's voice. "Where are you guys?"

"Here," cried David.

"But where?"

"Shine your light along the ground. I'll wave my hand."

A minute passed, then they heard Claire again. "I still can't see you."

"Hey, Jeff," said David. "I've got an idea. Maybe she'll see this." He pulled off his T-shirt, which was white. Then he wiggled it, bit by bit, up through the hole. The opening was just big enough for him to wave the shirt like a flag.

Finally, there was a steady beam of light, then the sound of running footsteps. A small hand clasped David's. "Is this you?" cried Claire.

"Yes, yes!" Next David felt the sniffing noses and slobbery tongues of three dogs.

"Rascal! Tessie! Hey, Jeff, the dogs are all here. Claire, what time is it?"

"Almost midnight."

"You're kidding!"

"Nope. Not kidding. We've got to hurry before our parents get home. Or else they'll ban us from here forever."

Jeff wanted to get down to business. "Claire," he shouted up to her, "you're amazing. We're so glad you're here. But we need you to guide us out of this cave. Are you okay? Are you scared?"

"I made it over here by myself, didn't I?"

"Right. Okay. Can you see our lookout tower?"

"Uh, hold on a minute. Yes. There's moonlight behind it."

Next, Jeff described how she could find the cave's entrance from the base of that tree.

"And you probably can see where we crawled under the bushes," David yelled. "The dirt is soft there."

"Got it," she said. "Tessie and Rascal will track you in no time. See you soon." Her footsteps crunched away.

They could hear Yum-Yum's bells grow faint once again.

"I can't believe it's the middle of the night."

"Me, neither. I hope we make it home before Mom does."

"How do you think Claire found us?" David wondered.

"Beats me. I'm just glad Uncle Wyatt taught her about boats. He's been letting her drive that outboard for months."

"She's smart all right."

"Yeah. And that dog of hers isn't so bad either."

# 17

# A Surprise

Jeff and David waited in the darkness for Claire. They finished the licorice while rubbing their arms to stay warm. Their canteens were now empty.

After some minutes, they heard a familiar noise. The panting of dogs and Yum-Yum's jingly collar echoed through the tunnel.

"Here, Tessie! Here, Rascal!" the brothers called. "Here, Yum-Yum." Suddenly they felt furry paws and wet noses. In the distance they could see Claire's light along the walls, moving toward them.

When she arrived, they were so relieved to see her they both talked at once.

"Guess what! The McCoys made it out here after all."

"We thought Mr. Wellback trapped us, but he didn't."

"How'd you get to the island, Claire?"

She told them about starting up the engine on her dad's little boat. "It's almost a full moon," she said, "so the lake is easy to see. I figured something had happened when you guys weren't home by sunset. The canoe wasn't at the dock. There were no lights on in your cabin. When you didn't answer your walkie-talkies, I knew I better get to the island.

"Anyway," she continued, "Tessie and Rascal led me to the lookout tower, but just sniffed around in circles. I was so glad when I finally saw your white flag!" Claire smiled at her cousins, but her expression quickly changed. "We gotta get going right now. Mom and Dad'll send out a search party if I'm not home when they get back from the café. It closes in less than an hour."

"We're ready!" said the brothers.

"Okay, follow me. Hey, it's *really* cold in here. Hold on a sec." As Claire zipped up her sweatshirt, her flashlight slipped from her hand. Now in the dark, she stumbled. There was a loud *snap* and *crackle* beneath her shoes. "Eew!" she cried. "What is *that*?"

David retrieved her flashlight and shone it toward her. When Claire saw what she had stepped on, she screamed and jumped away.

"Gruesome," Jeff said.

David's eyes were wide. "Wow."

# 18

# The Mystery Deepens

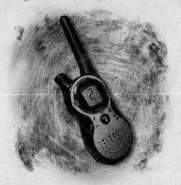

Claire had fallen over a human skeleton.

It was propped in a corner, as if sitting up, and Claire had tripped on the dead man's legs. Tatters of clothing were attached to the body. On the ground beside it was a valise, an old leather suitcase.

Claire was too startled to comment. She felt bad about having stepped on the bones but was still grossed out.

In the shadowy darkness, Jeff leaned close for a better look. "It's the bandit!" he cried. "He has two hands, but he's missing —"

"He's missing a foot," David finished. "So that was his foot we found. I *knew* that newspaper story got it wrong. Hey, maybe the gold's in that bag."

They turned the valise upside down. It was empty except for a broken pencil and a thin black book. David grabbed it, hoping there were drawings or a map inside. He held it to the flashlight and opened the crackly pages.

"Just lines full of numbers," he said, disappointed.

"So here lies the Silver Spur Bandit," said Jeff. "Too bad there's no money."

The cousins continued to gawk at the skeleton. For the moment, they forgot they were in a hurry. Then Claire said, "But what if the newspaper got it *right*? That it was the robber's hand that was shot off?"

"Then if this *isn't* the robber, who is it?" asked David.

"And why is he in this cave," Jeff said, "locked up in this room? I can't believe it's been in the corner this whole time with us in here! That creeps me out!"

"Me, too!" said David. "What if we'd fallen on it in the dark?"

The cousins wondered if they should say a prayer or a few words of kindness, like in the movies, but Claire reminded them of their situation. She pressed a button on her watch with her sparkly pink fingernail. The time glowed green.

"It's already 12:45!" she cried. "If we don't get home soon, we'll be in *so* much trouble."

In the tunnel, the cousins came upon two paths. One turned left, the other turned right.

"Claire?" said Jeff. "Do you remember which way you came in?"

Just then, another swarm of bats swooped overhead, the beating of their wings creating wind. Claire screamed. A foul odor made the cousins' eyes water.

"This place is *terrible*," Claire cried. "I can't believe you guys came in here without a plan." She swept her light back and forth. "There. Up ahead. We have to follow that."

"A golf ball?" David said. "Where'd it come from?"

"Remember the bucket of balls from your garage?"

"Hey, there's another one up there," said Jeff.

"It's a trail. Just like *Hansel and Gretel*," said Claire.

"Who?"

"You know, the story about the witch who lived in a forest and ate little children?" Claire asked, not pausing for a response. "Hansel and Gretel escaped because they had left stones along their path, all the way from their village. So when they ran out of the woods, they were able to find their way home. Come on, Jeff and David. We really gotta hurry."

David looked back at his brother. "Why didn't we think of that?"

"She's better at planning," said Jeff. "That's why."

# 19

# A New Theory

Claire's trail of golf balls led them out into the night.

The moon was setting behind the mountain. But because the sky was still aglow, the cousins were able to find their way through the woods to the beach. Jeff and David tied a rope to the canoe so they could tow it home. Then they watched as Claire started the outboard engine. The motorboat puttered across the lake under a canopy of stars.

When they reached the far shore, the cousins secured their crafts to the dock. The boys walked Claire and Yum-Yum to her cabin then ran home. After feeding their dogs, they hurried upstairs to their bedroom. From their window they saw headlights coming down the road from town. It was Aunt Lilly and Uncle Wyatt. Their jeep turned onto the driveway next door.

"Just in time," the brothers said. Now they crawled under their warm quilts. They were chilled after so many hours in the cave, and exhausted. While whispering about the skeleton, they fell sound asleep.

It was two o'clock in the morning. Soon

Mom would be driving home from her shift at the animal hospital.

The cousins slept in the next morning, they were so tired. For lunch they rode their bikes to the Western Café. They ordered burgers and fries for this important meeting.

Jeff began. "Well," he said, "we finally know that something really did happen on Lost Island. Whoever died in the cave was missing a foot and someone locked him in."

"And we found silver spurs," Claire said.

David was writing these clues in his sketchbook. "And we know the litterbug McCoys were on the island," he said. "Maybe they've even found the cave."

"Okay, what about the librarian?" Claire asked. "She didn't seem to care at all about the maps. But remember how nervous she was? She kept fidgeting and wouldn't look us in the eye. Was she just acting? Does she know something?"

David drew a giant Q on the page. He listed

his questions. "I wonder how Mr. Wellback knew the maps were missing. Remember how he said we wouldn't find anything in the atlases? And why was he spying on us from the dock yesterday? Another thing — why does he fake a limp? We saw him carrying all that lumber, and he wasn't limping then."

"And why doesn't he want us on Lost Island?" Claire asked.

"Maybe his old grandpa sheriff buried some gold out there," Jeff replied, "and told his family about it. Now all these years later, Grumpy Gus wants to find it before we do."

The cousins were quiet, pondering these theories. They passed around ketchup for their fries. Claire gave Jeff her pickle. He gave her his lettuce and tomato. While David was looking under the table for his napkin, they quickly transferred their black olives to his plate.

The napkin found, David used it to wipe the mayonnaise off his bun.

A waitress brought three milk shakes to their booth. She was an older lady with curly gray hair. "Kids," she said, "I couldn't help but overhear you discussing Grumpy Gus. That old man has been trying for years to prove his ancestor was an honest sheriff, but no one believes him. He's just trying to make himself look good by clearing the family name, that's all. You better stay away from the old coot."

She gave them extra napkins then left. Not until she went behind the counter did anyone say a word.

Jeff looked over his shoulder to make sure people at the next table weren't listening. In a low voice he said, "Now what about the skeleton? When should we tell the police?"

"Today," was Claire's quick answer. "Before Rex and Ronald find it and do something to it. You said you found the candy wrapper by the cave's entrance, right? So they probably know how to get inside."

David frowned. "So if we tell the police about the skeleton, what happens to Fort Grizzly Paw? It won't be a secret anymore with cops swarming around. They'll tell their kids, then everyone in Cabin Creek will know."

The cousins looked out the window, again thoughtful. It was a hot afternoon. They could see the lake. A swimmers' beach was there and a dock with paddleboats. Teenagers were playing volleyball in the sand. Others were

Rollerblading, some had skateboards. A basketball court was busy.

Jeff poked a straw into his shake then took a loud slurp. "Maybe it won't be so bad. Lost Island is far away and hard to find. And except for the McCoys, not that many kids have their own boats for getting there."

"Plus," Claire said, "there's tons of stuff for kids to do here in town. No one cares about Lost Island like we do."

David grinned. "That's for ding-dong sure." Even though he was suspicious of Mr. Wellback, he liked how the old man said things.

## 20

# The Police Station

After lunch, the cousins rode through town to the police station. The captain listened to their story. He studied David's drawing of the skeleton, which he had sketched from memory. Just for fun, David had added a spider crawling over the skull, and also a rat sitting on the bony shoulder.

"This is quite good, young fellow," the man said. "All my life I've wondered if there was any truth to that legend. And now we might have some evidence." He tipped back his chair to gaze out the window. The view of Blue Mountain and the lake was like a postcard.

The cousins waited while the captain seemed lost in memory. His eyes were dreamy and he had a slight smile. This is when they noticed a woman in the next office, working at a computer. She seemed familiar.

"*The librarian!*" Claire whispered, nudging Jeff and David. "She works here, too."

Suddenly the captain sat up, as if he had been caught napping. "What's that you say?" When he saw the children staring, he said, "Oh, she's my sister. Helps me out on Fridays. Do you know her?"

The cousins looked at one another, careful

about what to say. "Only that she's the new librarian," Jeff replied. "We saw her the other day."

"Heavens," the man said. "Poor girl had to quit after her first day. She was so allergic to dust from the old books, her eyes stung and stung. She couldn't even see straight. It's too bad, too. She's new in town and it would've given her a chance to make friends. Now, where were we? Oh, yes. We have some business to take care of. I know the museum director will be interested in the spurs you found, but too bad there's no money to divvy up. Anyhow, we need your help guiding investigators into that cave. I'll speak with your parents. If it's okay with them, can you kids meet our team at the island next Wednesday morning? Say, nine o'clock?"

"Yes, sir," replied Jeff.

"You'll see our red canoe on the north shore," David said.

"And our dogs," added Claire. "They're very suspicious of strangers, so don't make any sudden moves." Claire had heard this line in a movie and liked its dramatic effect.

As the cousins rode away from the police station, they discussed the grouchy woman from the library, the captain's sister.

"Since she has allergies," Claire said, "that explains why she was rubbing her nose and blinking. Those atlases are really old and dusty."

"And maybe she was nervous because it was her first day," David suggested.

"We *were* whispering a lot," Jeff said. "Maybe that's why she was staring at us."

Continuing home, they passed the park and baseball field. Behind the library, they came to an empty lot with a handmade sign: COMMUNITY GARDEN. They were surprised to see Mr. Wellback there with a hoe and wheelbarrow. He was resting on a bench. In front of him were rows of dirt, dotted with tiny green plants. Signs at the end of each row had pictures of vegetables, such as corn, peppers, carrots, and cucumbers.

The cousins got off their bikes and leaned them against a tree. A small ice chest was there in the shade.

"Hello, Mr. Gus," they called. They did not plan to ignore him, as the waitress had advised.

The old man hobbled toward them to cool off under the tree. "My bones get all cricky if I sit too long," he told them. "But once I get going, why, I can outwalk a dog and probably you rascals. Well, I sure could've used your help yesterday. Took hours to build these."

Mr. Wellback pointed to several large flower boxes. Inside these boxes were tall sticks with rope stretched between them like spiderwebs. They formed a type of trellis, where vines from beans and squash could grow.

When the cousins saw the rope and freshly cut lumber, they glanced at one another with sorry looks. They already had realized Mr. Wellback didn't make the door in the cave to trap the boys. But it hadn't occurred to them he might be building something nice for the town. They felt ashamed.

"All right," he said, "since we're standing around twiddling our thumbs, we may as well celebrate."

"Celebrate?" they asked.

Without answering, Mr. Wellback bent down to open the ice chest. Out came a package of graham crackers, a carton of cold orange juice, and some paper cups. He passed these around. Then he looked up at the sky.

"Well, back when I was a boy," he said, "I had a terrible sadness. So every day from then on, I would find something interesting to look at. Something to make me feel better. Today it's that fluffy white cloud over the mountain. See it sitting there? Pretty, isn't it? Well, five minutes from now, it'll drift into a new shape. Then its shadow will float over the forest."

He sat on the ice chest. "To me, that's worth celebrating."

The cousins and old man sat in the shade, watching the sky. They drank orange juice and ate graham crackers. After a while, he put his hands on his knees and said, "Okay. Time to get back to work. My cricky bones need to move. You scallywag kids run along now."

"Thank you, Mr. Gus," Claire replied.

"Yes, thank you," said the boys.

"Well, off you go," he said. "And don't forget what I told you about Lost Island. You steer clear of that place. The last time your dad and I went hiking together, I promised him I'd always watch over you."

At the mention of their father, Jeff and David turned around. "You went hiking with our dad?" Jeff asked.

"All the time," the man answered. "Went backpacking in the wilderness every summer before you tadpoles were born. Friends can really listen to each other out there. Didn't he tell you about our adventures?"

David squinted as he thought. "He told us about hiking with his friend Mr. Penny, but we never met him. There are lots of families around here with that name."

Mr. Wellback coughed as if he were trying not to laugh. "In school do you rascally kids do your math homework?"

They hesitated. "Sort of," they said.

"Can you add?"

"That's the easiest," said David.

Now it was Mr. Wellback's turn to squint, looking them each in the eye. "All right, then," he said. "Add Mr. Penny to Mr. Gus and what do you have?"

Claire opened her mouth in surprise. "Your name is Gus Penny? Of course, like the old gunslinger sheriff."

He laughed again. "Well, I'm not Pope Peter, that's for ding-dong sure."

Jeff and David were stunned. Suddenly the loss of their father had been softened. They were looking into the eyes of his old friend.

"We saw you on our dock yesterday," Jeff said. "With binoculars."

"Well, how else can I keep an eye on you mischief-makers? Was on my way out of town to visit my sister. When I came back this morning, first thing I did was look for your red canoe. That's how I know you got home safe. Any more questions? You're wearing me out."

"No, sir."

# 21

# The Missing Clue

Wednesday morning, the cousins canoed to Lost Island to meet the investigators. They had dressed up for the occasion. The brothers were in their favorite T-shirts, even though David's happened to be inside out again with the tag in front. Claire's shorts and shirt were purple, and her blue sneakers had yellow laces. Yum-Yum matched in a little purple jacket with blue bows on her ears.

Even Tessie and Rascal were fancy. They

wore matching red bandannas around their necks and had been freshly brushed.

While they waited on shore for the officials, the cousins discussed Mr. Wellback.

"I feel awful," said Jeff. "Dad always talked about his hiking buddy, Mr. Penny, but we didn't know he and Mr. Wellback were the same person. And all this time, we thought he was a bad guy."

"I feel bad for suspecting him," David said. "He's kind of like a mystery, all by himself. I wonder what Mr. Wellback meant when he said he had sadness as a boy."

"Yeah. *Terrible* sadness," Claire corrected.

The investigators arrived two hours late. Their boats had gotten lost among the forested inlets, and they had circled the wrong islands. When they arrived, a history professor from the university announced that she was in charge. She wore hiking boots and a ranger hat.

"Shall we?" the professor said to the children. She didn't apologize for being late, but motioned for them to lead the way.

A dozen adults with flashlights and headlamps followed the kids into the cave. Claire's golf balls were still there. The cousins had secured them with mud and glue a few days earlier.

The professor held a lantern over the skeleton to examine it. She groaned. "Oh, for crying out loud! It's missing a *foot*, not a *hand*. I thought you said this was the Silver Spur Bandit."

"We did," began Jeff. He was going to explain about mistakes in newspapers, but she interrupted him.

"And what is *this* doing here?" She picked up a candy wrapper and waved it in front of their flashlight. "It's called litter, that's what. Don't you kids know anything about being responsible?"

The cousins were too surprised to answer — and too disappointed. This wrapper was evidence the McCoys had found their way into this part of the cave. Lost Island would never be the same with Rex and Ronald hanging around.

Then two interesting things happened:

First, the woman looked in the valise. She pulled out the pencil and, in frustration, turned the bag upside down. "What? Nothing but a rotten old pencil?"

In the bumpy shadows of the cave, the children could see the professor glaring at them. But Claire was thinking, *Did the McCoys take that little black book?*

The second interesting thing was this: When the men gathered the bones, they didn't notice that something rolled from the skeleton's ragged shirt onto the ground. It landed with a quiet *plop*. Only the cousins saw. Quick as a wink, Jeff stepped on it. After he hid it in his pocket, they followed the adults out into the sunlight.

Claire and David were bursting to know what Jeff had picked up, but they stayed silent.

*　　*　　*

Outside, the woman slapped her notebook closed. "If this had been the Silver Spur Bandit," she said, looking down at the children, "I could have written a book and you would've been famous. But there's no story here. This was probably some old fool who went off the deep end and locked himself in the cave." The professor sighed with impatience.

"A complete waste of my time." She put on her sunglasses and marched down to the beach. A man in a dinghy motored her out to a speedboat that was anchored offshore. She was the last of her team and equipment to board. The boat sped away, its engine loud and splashy. Soon it was a dot on the vast lake.

Immediately, the cousins took off their shoes to wade in the cool water. They splashed one another and jabbered.

"What did you find, Jeff? Show us!"

From his pocket, Jeff pulled out a brownish-yellow coin. "I wasn't sure what it was," he said, "but I thought I better get it. I wonder if it's —"

"Is it gold?" Claire and David cried.

The older boy brushed off the coin, then bit down on it as he'd seen cowboys do in the movies. "Hard as rock," he said with a smile.

"Yes!" The kids jumped in the air with high fives, such was their excitement. "There's probably more somewhere!"

"But not if the McCoys found it," Jeff said.

David shook his head and kicked at the water. "I can't believe they found the cave."

"And that they left trash, as usual!" Claire said.

"And not to mention they stole the little black book!"

At this, David stopped splashing. "Guys," he said. "I have to tell you something."

# 22

# The Ledger

David went up to the dry sand for his pack. He pulled out the waterproof case with his sketchbook and colored pencils. He opened it and held up the little black book.

"I didn't mean to keep it a secret," he said. "That night in the cave, I was still holding it when we had to hurry out. I just forgot."

"No big deal," said Jeff.

Claire agreed. "At least you kept it safe, David. We can give it to the police later. Better than the McCoys or that snooty professor getting it."

After they cleaned up their orange peels and baggies from lunch, the boys played with the dogs. They threw sticks for them while Claire sat on the beach. She wanted to look at the book again before they gave it to the police. Now that they knew the skeleton wasn't the Silver Spur Bandit, they had no idea whose book it was.

The first pages were columns of numbers, dated 1882. *An old ledger*, she thought. It was similar to one her parents used to keep track of money in the café. However, something caught her eye. As Claire turned the brittle pages, she noticed words scrawled between the rows of numbers. Some were faded, some smudged. But soon she realized it was a letter.

TO WHOM IT MAY CONCERN:

I, AUGUSTUS PENNY, SHERIFF OF CABIN CREEK & ENVIRONS, DO WRITE THESE FINAL WORDS. TO RECOUNT THE PAST FIVE DAYS: POSSE & I TRACKED THE WELLS FARGO THIEF TO LOST ISLAND. DESPITE HIS WOUNDED HAND, HIS GOOD AIM WITH HIS SIX-SHOOTER CAUSED MY FOOT TO BE BLOWN OFF. NOW CRIPPLED AND LOSING BLOOD FAST, I MADE A TORCH FROM THE BANDIT'S CAMPFIRE. THUS ON HANDS &

KNEES, I FOLLOWED HIS BLOODY TRAIL INTO THIS CAVE.

ALAS, THE DIRE NEWS IS NOT THAT I SHALL NEVERMORE SEE THE LIGHT OF DAY — FOR I AM READY TO MEET MY MAKER — BUT THAT MY DEPUTIES ARE TRAITORS. ONE SIGHT OF ALL THAT GOLD & THEY CIRCLED LIKE STARVING WOLVES. AT THIS MOMENT THEY — AND THEIR NEW FRIEND THE BANDIT — ARE HAMMERING A CRUDE DOOR TO ENSURE I DON'T COME AFTER THEM. THEY HAVE LEFT ME HERE WITH ONE CANDLE & THIS BANK LEDGER. 'TIS A FEEBLE JOKE ON THEIR PART, HOWEVER, BECAUSE I HAVE THE LAST LAUGH. THEY DON'T KNOW THAT DESPITE THE LOSS OF MY FOOT, I WAS ABLE TO RECOVER SOME ~~JEWELRY~~ &

HID THEM NEAR ~~A QUARTER TREE~~. TO MY THREE BROTHERS, I HOPE YOU CATCH THOSE FOULEST OF FOUL MEN & FIND THE REST OF THE ~~VALUES~~. TO MY BELOVED WIFE AND CHILDREN, KNOW THAT MY LAST BREATH WILL WHISPER YOUR NAMES. ALAS, CANDLE IS

Claire closed the little book. She sighed. She was only nine years old, but her heart ached for the good sheriff alone in the cave. And for his wife and children who never learned the noble truth. *We have to give this to Mr. Wellback*, she thought.

Claire couldn't wait to tell her cousins the true identity of the skeleton. But when she returned the ledger to David's bag, she noticed something else.

"David," she called. He and Jeff were still splashing in the lake with the dogs.

"Yeah?" he said.

"David, where do you put your lunch wrappers?"

"Side pocket in my pack," he called. "Then I take them home to throw them away." He threw a stick in shallow water so old Tessie wouldn't have to swim too far.

"David?" she again called.

"*What?*"

Claire was holding up his backpack. Her hand was in the side pouch with her fingers sticking out the bottom.

"There's a gigantic hole, David Bridger. *You're* the litterbug of Lost Island!"

# 23

# Two Gifts

Mr. Wellback closed the ledger and removed his spectacles. He rubbed his eyes and looked off toward the lake. The cousins were sitting with him on his shaded porch, the dogs asleep at their feet. A pitcher of water and paper cups were on a bench beside them.

Rubbing his eyes again he said, "My good friend Russell — that's your dad, boys — he always believed the sheriff, my grandfather Penny, was innocent. Said he'd prove it one day, so my family could rest in peace. Lord knows, I had given up on trying. But you three did it for him." He cleared his throat, again looking away. His white hair was fluffed up like a dandelion.

Jeff realized Mr. Wellback was feeling emotional so it didn't surprise him when his father's friend changed the subject. "Well, what d'you know!" the man exclaimed. "It's hot as blazes out here! Be sure you drink enough water in this high altitude, or else you'll get a headache." He paused and looked again at his guests. "Sonny, there's a question on your face."

"Yes, sir," answered David. "How did you know we wouldn't find those maps to Lost Island in the library?"

"Hooligans!" was his quick reply. "Back when I was your age, a band of kids stole 'em. No respect for books. They played hooky to go treasure hunting with those maps. They accused my ancestor of running away with the loot, but I never believed that part of the legend. So one afternoon, I went to Lost Island with my good dog, Bunny, to search on my own. Didn't tell my folks or anyone."

Mr. Wellback took a long drink of water. He wiped his moustache, then his beard. "Where was I?"

"Your dog, Bunny."

"Oh, yes. In those days, a spit of land connected the island to Grizzly Paw Wilderness, so moose, bears, and mountain lions went back and forth. Was a dangerous place." The old man looked down at his rough hands. "Well, back then I was a foolish lad. I was tired from searching the island and went to sleep in my tent with a bag of ham sandwiches. A grizzly came in the night, hungry, and tore through the tent like it was paper. His claws slashed my leg and he would've finished me off except for Bunny jumping at his throat."

Mr. Wellback set his cup down. "Saved my life, she did. But the griz carried her off. I was alone and bleeding, couldn't walk. At last I was able to get a campfire going. My big brother saw the smoke two days later and found me. Leg still aches . . ." His voice trailed off.

Claire looked at him thoughtfully. "Is that your terrible sadness?" she asked. "Because of your dog, Bunny?"

The man closed his eyes.

The cousins were quiet, thinking of their own beloved pets.

"Sir?" It was Claire again. "Why do you tell us to stay away from Lost Island?"

Mr. Wellback took a deep breath and leaned forward. "I don't want the same thing to happen to you children or your dogs."

The cousins nodded with understanding.

"Another thing," he continued, "this lake is dangerous when a wind comes up. You ought to be more careful. Any more questions?"

"No, sir."

Jeff reached into his pocket and handed Mr. Wellback the coin. "We think your long-ago grandpa would be glad for you to have this. It fell out of his shirt."

"It should be yours," Claire and David agreed.

The old man put on his glasses. He read the coin's bumpy surface. "Why, this is a twenty-dollar gold piece. You sure about this?"

"We're sure."

A minute passed. "All right, then," said Mr. Wellback. "I might need to contact Wells Fargo, to see if it's legal for me to keep it. After all, it was their stagecoach the bandit robbed. But first, let's celebrate." He poured water for the children, then a cup for himself. They sat on his porch listening to the creek that flowed nearby and the wind high up in the trees. They waited for Mr. Wellback to say something else.

Finally the old man stood up. "Guess I need some thinking time. You scallywags run along now." He waved his arm as if shooing chickens off his porch.

"Bye, Mr. Penny. Thanks for everything."

When they were on the dirt road, he called from his porch. "Listen to your folks now and don't scare them with any foolishness."

The cousins and their dogs followed the stream down from Mr. Wellback's cabin. They felt good to have helped him learn the truth about his ancestor.

Jeff picked up a flat little rock. He leaned low and flicked it toward the stream, where it skipped several times across the water.

"Hey, guys," Jeff said, picking up another stone. "Remember what the old sheriff said in his letter? That he had fooled the bandit and his deputies? And that he hid something somewhere?"

"Yeah," agreed David. "I bet there's more treasure to find."

"Well, what are we waiting for?" Claire asked. "Summer's just begun!"

GET A SNEAK PEEK AT
JEFF, DAVID, AND CLAIRE'S
NEXT EXCITING ADVENTURE:

# THE CLUE AT THE
# BOTTOM OF THE LAKE

# The Clue at the Bottom
# of the Lake

①

# A Mysterious Splash

The Scottish terrier growled low in his throat. His front paws were on the windowsill as he looked out at the darkness. It was the middle of the night.

Twelve-year-old Jeff Bridger bolted awake, immediately concerned.

"What is it, Rascal?" he whispered.

Through the open bedroom window came the sputtering of a motorboat on the lake. Jeff squinted at the digital clock. What was anyone doing out there at two-thirty in the morning?

He grabbed his binoculars from his bedpost. Then he jumped up to wake his ten-year-old brother, David, who was wrapped in his quilt on the floor. Tessie, their old yellow Lab, was stretched out on David's bed as usual, her head on the pillow. Not bothered by minor disturbances, Tessie slept on.

"David, look! Hurry! A boat's at the island. Something's not right."

David popped up. Still in his T-shirt and shorts from yesterday, he was ready for action. "Okay. I'm awake." He found his binoculars among the clutter of socks and shoes beside him.

In the starlight, the brothers could see Lost Island. Their secret fort was hidden in the island's forest, but they weren't concerned with the fort now. Circling near the rocky point was an aluminum fishing boat that had a shiny stripe along its side. Someone was in the bow, holding up a lantern — the boys couldn't tell if it was a man or a woman. The engine had slowed to a *putter . . . putter . . . putter*.

Suddenly, a large object was rolled over the side. It splashed into the black water and sank from view. Though half a mile across the lake, the noise was as loud as if from their kitchen downstairs. Jeff and David looked at each other, then raised their binoculars again. Now the boat had been pulled ashore, and someone was walking on the island.

Jeff lowered his voice so he wouldn't wake their mother. "Did that look like someone threw a body overboard?" he asked his younger brother.

"Definitely."

They listened until once again the night was still. Stars wiggled on the surface of the dark lake. Though it seemed peaceful, the boys were uneasy. Jeff reached over a Monopoly game scattered on the carpet for his walkie-talkie.

"We have to let Claire know." He clicked a dial, then held down a button. "Claire?" he whispered into the speaker. "Wake up. Over." He paused a moment, then repeated his message.

Claire was their nine-year-old cousin and best friend. She, too, lived on the lake. Her log home was close enough to Jeff and David's that they could signal each other from their bedroom windows. A footbridge over the creek connected the two properties. When they wanted to talk late at night, the cousins used two-way radios turned down low, so they wouldn't bother their parents. They wished they had cell phones, but there was no reception in these mountains.

Soon, a girl's voice came through the static. "Claire Posey reporting for duty. What's up, guys? Over."

"Suspicious activity," said Jeff. "Will debrief tomorrow. Come to breakfast at seven o'clock. Over." He and his brother liked to use military time.

"Jeff, we were already planning to make pancakes together, remember? Over."

"Oh, right. I forgot. See you tomorrow, then. Over." To David he said, "Now do the secret code."

David aimed his flashlight at Claire's window. He waved it around, then turned it off and on several times. In response, Claire tugged the strings on her venetian blinds: Open. Shut. Open. Twice. Then, for a grand finale, David smooshed his face against the glass, shining his light up through his nose. At that, Claire closed her blinds.

"What code did you give her?" Jeff asked, getting back into bed.

"Oh, the usual."

"You mean, you made something up?"

"Yep." David returned to his nest on the floor and rolled into his quilt. "Hey, Jeff, what if that really was a body?"

Jeff checked under his pillow to make sure his flashlight was still there. "Well, if it is a body," he replied, "then someone was murdered."